WHAT IS AN EASY READER?

- This story has been carefully written to capture the interest of the young reader.

- It is told in a simple, direct style with a strong rhythm that adds enjoyment both to reading aloud and silent reading.

- Many key words are repeated regularly throughout the story. This skillful repetition helps the child to read independently. Encountering words again and again, the young reader practices the vocabulary he or she knows, and learns with ease the words that are new.

- Only 167 words have been used, with plurals and root words counted once.

  Over one-half of the total vocabulary has been used at least three times.

  One-third of the total vocabulary has been used at least six times.

  Some words have been used 15, 18 and 31 times.

ABOUT THIS STORY

- Kittens are a beloved subject of young readers, and here, in an easy-to-read story, they will meet four of them. Youngsters will like the joke, too.

  This story will serve as a good introduction to conversation about, or the study of, pets.

One kitten is not too many

Story *by* DOROTHY LEVENSON
Pictures *by* CARL *and* MARY HAUGE
Editorial Consultant: LILIAN MOORE

Wonder® Books
PRICE/STERN/SLOAN
Publishers, Inc., Los Angeles
1987

Introduction

Easy Readers help young readers discover what a delightful experience reading can be. The stories are such fun that they inspire children to try new reading skills. They are so easy to read that they provide encouragement and support for children as readers.

The adult will notice that the sentences aren't too long, the words aren't too hard, and the skillful repetition is like a helping hand. What the child will feel is: "This is a good story—and I can read it myself!"

For some children, the best way to meet these stories may be to hear them read aloud at first. Others, who are better prepared to read on their own, may need a little help in the beginning—help that is best given freely. Youngsters who have more experience in reading alone—whether in first or second or third grade—will have the immediate joy of reading "all by myself."

These books have been planned to help all young readers grow—in their pleasure in books and in their power to read them.

Lilian Moore
Specialist in Reading
Formerly of Division of Instructional Research,
New York City Board of Education

SECOND PRINTING — APRIL 1987

Copyright © 1964, 1981 by Price/Stern/Sloan Publishers, Inc.
Cover Copyright © 1986 Price/Stern/Sloan Publishers, Inc.
Published by Price/Stern/Sloan Publishers, Inc.
360 North La Cienega Boulevard, Los Angeles, California 90048

ISBN: 0-8431-4316-9

Wonder Books® is a trademark of Price/Stern/Sloan Publishers, Inc.

This is Fat Cat.

She is big and fat and sleepy.

She lives with the Dooley family.

This is Mrs. Dooley.

This is Mr. Dooley.

This is Sue.

And this is Mary.

One day Fat Cat had kittens.

One, two, three,

four kittens.

9

The kittens were not big.

They were not fat.

And they were NOT sleepy.

They liked to run and jump.

They ran upstairs and downstairs.

They jumped up and down

and in and out.

They seemed to be everywhere.

There was a kitten here.

There was a kitten there.

12

And here . . .

. . . and there.

Mr. Dooley found a kitten in his hat.

He found a kitten in his bed.

He found a kitten on his books.

At last he said:

"We have too many kittens!

They must go!"

"Oh, no!" cried Sue.

"Oh, Daddy, no!" cried Mary.

"Oh, no, dear!" said Mrs. Dooley.

"Well, look at them!"

said Mr. Dooley.

"Get away from there!" he cried,

and he ran after the kittens.

"Out they go!" he said again.

"Four kittens are too many!"

"Please, Daddy!" said Sue.

"Please!" said Mary.

"Please, dear!" said Mrs. Dooley.

"All right! All right!"

said Mr. Dooley.

"But next time . . . !"

That night Mr. Dooley
came home a little late.
"What are we having for supper?"
he said.
"I'm hungry."

"I made fish for supper,"
said Mrs. Dooley.

"Good," said Mr. Dooley.
"I do like fish.
Let's have supper right away."

So the family sat right down

for supper.

But where was the fish?

Not on the dish.

Not on the table.

The kittens had the fish.

They liked it, too!

"Oh!" said Mary.

"Oh, look!" said Sue.

"Oh, my!" said Mrs. Dooley.

"OH, NO!" said Mr. Dooley.

"My supper! My fish!

Out those kittens go! Right now!"

Mr. Dooley got a big box.

Then he ran after the kittens.

"Here, kitty . . . kitty!" he cried.

At last Mr. Dooley

had the four kittens.

He put them in the box.

The kittens cried for Fat Cat.

Fat Cat cried for her kittens.

Mary cried.

Sue cried.

Mrs. Dooley cried.

But Mr. Dooley said:

"Too many kittens!

Out they go!"

Mr. Dooley took the kittens
away in the box.

He took them all the way to
Mr. Brown's pet store.

"Oh, KITTENS!" said Mr. Brown.

"Yes, I will take them.

Everyone likes kittens.

I can sell them all."

Mr. Brown put the kittens

in the window of his store.

The next day Sue went to school.

On the way she went past
the pet store.

There were the four kittens
in the window.

On the way home Sue went past
the pet store again.
There were the four kittens.
Sue looked at them again.

Then she said:

"One kitten is not too many."

Sue went into the pet store
and she came out with one kitten.
Sue ran all the way home.
But she did not tell anyone
about the kitten.
"I will keep it a surprise
for after supper," she said.

Mary went past the pet store

on the way to school.

She saw the kittens, too.

On the way home

she stopped to look again.

"Oh," she said,

"now there are only three!"

Mary went into the pet store.

"Hi!" said Mr. Brown.

"Hi!" said Mary.

"I want to buy one kitten, please.

One kitten is not too many, is it?"

"Oh, no," said Mr. Brown.

"One kitten is just right."

Mary ran all the way home.
But she did not tell anyone
about the kitten.
"I will keep it a surprise
for after supper," she said.

She put the kitten in her room.

That day Mrs. Dooley

went past the pet store.

She saw two kittens in the window.

Mrs. Dooley went into the store.

"Good day," she said.

"It is a good day," said Mr. Brown.

"A very good day
for selling kittens."

"That's just what I want,"
said Mrs. Dooley.

"One kitten, please.
After all, one kitten
is not too many."

Mrs. Dooley took the kitten home.

She put the kitten in her room.

"I will keep it a surprise

for after supper," she said.

On his way home Mr. Dooley went
past the pet store.

He saw one kitten in the window.

"My!" he said.

"There is just one kitten now.

One kitten is not too many."

So Mr. Dooley went into the store.

MR. BROWN'S
Pet Store

MR. BROU
Pet St

He came out with a kitten—
one kitten.

"I will keep it a surprise
for after supper," he said.
He put his kitten in a box.

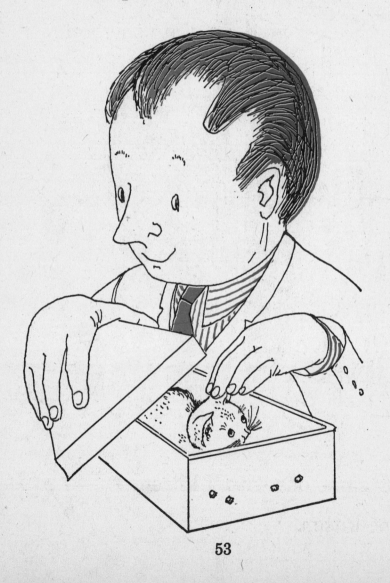

Soon it was supper time.

The Dooleys all sat down to eat.

Mrs. Dooley said:

"I must give Fat Cat some milk."

She put some milk in a dish
and said: "Here kitty, kitty!"

Fat Cat came.

But so did the kittens!

One kitten,

two kittens,

three kittens,

four kittens—

they all came running!

"Oh, no!" said Mr. Dooley.

"KITTENS!

How did they all get here?"

Sue said: "I got one kitten. . ."

And Mary said: "So did I!"

Mrs. Dooley said: "So did I!"

"And," said Mr. Dooley, "so did I!"

They all looked at Mr. Dooley.

He looked at the four kittens.

Then Mr. Dooley began to laugh.

"Well," he said,

"one kitten is not too many,

so we will keep one kitten.

One kitten for Sue.

One kitten for Mary.

One kitten for Mother.

And one kitten for me!"